For Guthrie, Doris, Elizabeth and Tony,
17 Christmases together.
With love, Pa x

T. M.

For cheeky young Theo and Tegan.
Merry Christmas!

L. M.

ORCHARD BOOKS
338 Euston Road, London, NW1 3BH
Orchard Books Australia
Level 17/207 Kent Street, Sydney, NSW 2000

First published in 2007 by Orchard Books
ISBN 978 1 84362 876 7

Text © Tony Mitton 2007
Illustrations © Layn Marlow 2007

The right of Tony Mitton to be identified as the author
and of Layn Marlow as the illustrator of this work has been asserted
by them in accordance with the Copyright, Designs and Patents Act, 1988.
A CIP catalogue record for this book is available from the British Library.

1 3 5 7 9 10 8 6 4 2

Printed in Singapore

Orchard Books is a division of Hachette Children's Books,
an Hachette Livre UK company.

Tony Mitton   Layn Marlow

Christmas Wishes

ORCHARD BOOKS

On the night before Christmas,
the tree was all hung
With lights and with baubles
that shone as they swung.

The branches were dangled
with glittering things,
While the fairy perched high
with her wand and her wings.

There were presents wrapped shinily
under the tree.
There were green leaves and berries
and cards hung to see.

For at last it was Christmas!
And late Christmas Eve
Is when Santa Claus visits,
or so folk believe.

So we set out a drink
and a Christmassy snack,
With a note saying, "Santa,
please put down your sack . . .

And nibble some Christmas cake,
  give it a try!
For it must be so cold
  in the midwinter sky.

And here are some carrots,
  so crunchy and sweet.
Your hardworking reindeer
  could do with a treat."

Then Dad told a story
and Mum sang a song,
And soon it was time
to be getting along.

So we hung up our stockings
and went to our beds,

As thoughts of our presents
swam round in our heads.

We lay in our beds
   as the minutes went by,
But all we could do
   was to wriggle and sigh.

To stay up at Christmas
   just couldn't be right.
But in through our window,
   the moon shone so bright.

It must have been later
than midnight, I guess,
And our heads were all hot
and our beds were a mess,

When outside the window
we heard a faint jingle,
Which made our hearts leap
and our skin start to tingle.

We crept to the window
and stood on the ledge,
And spied in the sky . . .

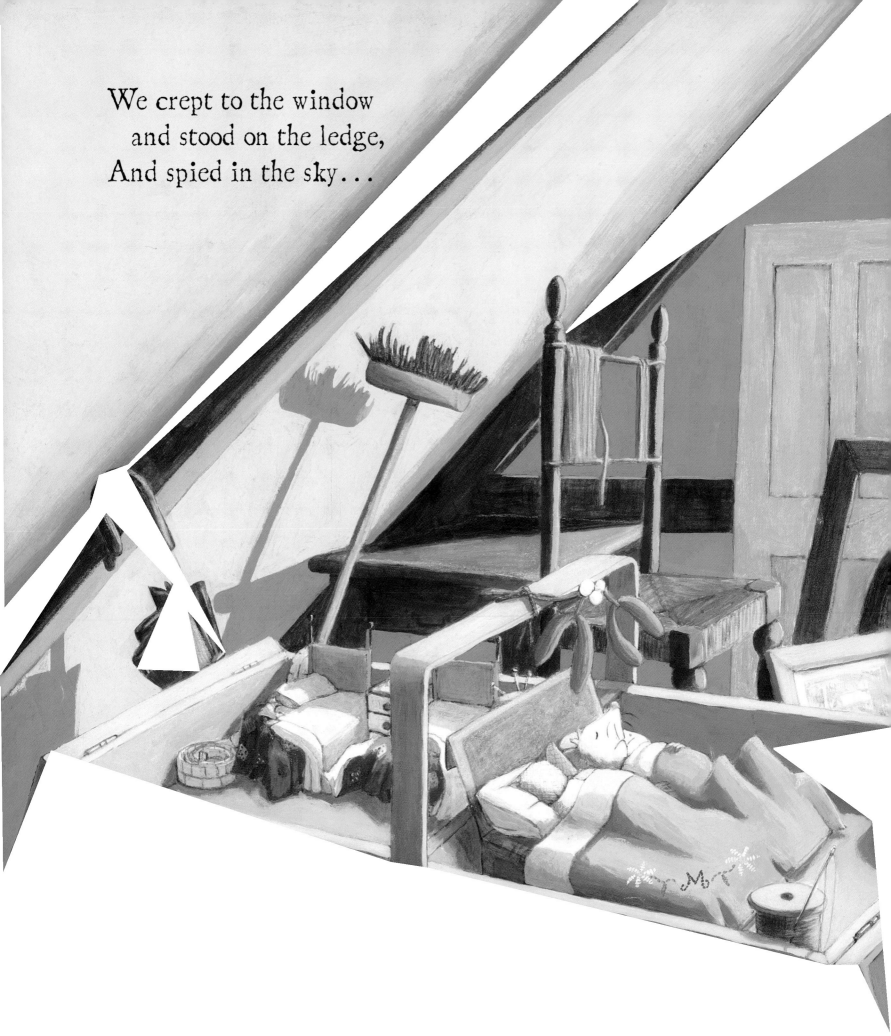

... an incredible sledge!

It was pulled by eight reindeer.
The first had a nose
That glowed quite as brightly
as any red rose!

The sledge had a cargo
   of sacks piled up high,
Which the reindeer had cantered
   across the night sky.

And there, as we watched it,
the driver leaned out,
As both of us struggled
to hold back a shout.

His suit was bright red
and his beard was white.
"It's Santa!" we whispered,
with gasps of delight.

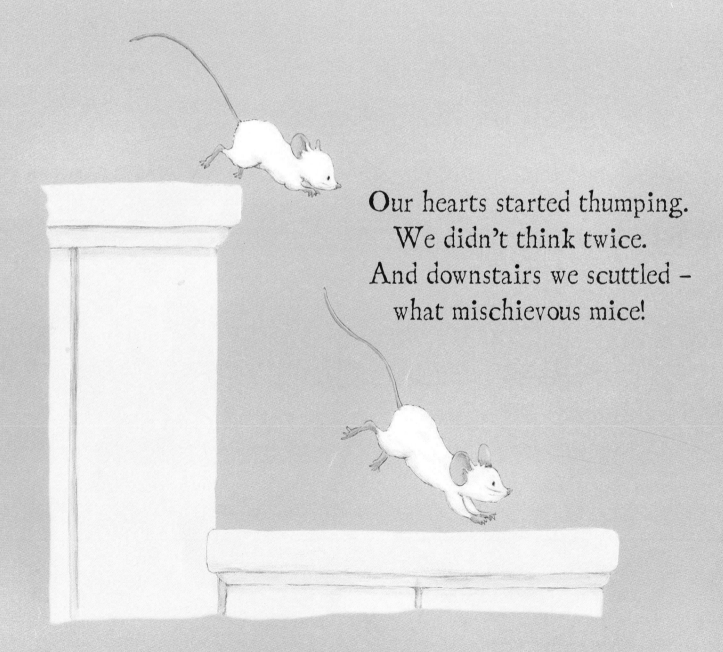

Our hearts started thumping.
We didn't think twice.
And downstairs we scuttled –
what mischievous mice!

Old Santa had come down
    the chimney, and now
He was wiping the soot
    from his beard and his brow.

He read all our messages,
    mumbled, "Let's see ..."
Then he filled up our stockings
    and chuckled with glee.

He nibbled some cake,
   and then, what do you think?
He turned round to face us
   and gave us a wink!

He waggled a finger,
   but smiled as he said,
"What cheeky young children!
   Be off now! To bed!"

There was nothing to answer.
   No, nothing to say.
We knew it was true,
   so we had to obey.

We scuttled back up
   to our window, amazed,
To catch a last glimpse,
   and we gazed and we gazed.

Old Santa was giving
   his reindeer a munch
Of the carrots we'd left,
   and some apples to crunch.

Then he reached for the reins
as he jumped in the sleigh,
And he called with a chuckle,
"Now, up and away!"

The reindeer clawed hard
at the air with their hoofs,
Till the sleigh slowly rose
to the height of the roofs.

And Santa waved down
with a cry of delight . . .

"Merry Christmas, my dears . . .

and a very good night!"